D0801611

BRATS

SOME OTHER BOOKS BY X. J. KENNEDY

The Forgetful Wishing Well: POEMS FOR YOUNG PEOPLE
The Owlstone Crown
(Margaret K. McElderry Books)

Knock at a Star: A CHILD'S INTRODUCTION TO POETRY
(with Dorothy M. Kennedy)
Did Adam Name the Vinegarroon?

BRATS

X. J. KENNEDY

illustrations by James Watts

A Margaret K. McElderry Book
ATHENEUM   1986   NEW YORK

LIBRARY OF CONGRESS CATALOGING-IN-PUBLICATION DATA
Kennedy, X. J.
    Brats.

    "A Margaret K. McElderry book."
    Summary: Forty-two poems describe a variety of
particularly unpleasant brats.
        1. Discipline of children — Juvenile poetry.
2. Children's poetry, American.   [1. Behavior — Poetry.
2. American poetry]   I. Title.
PS3521.E563B68   1986   811'.54   85-20018
ISBN 0-689-50392-X

Published simultaneously in Canada by Collier Macmillan Canada, Inc.
Composition by Maryland Linotype Composition Company
Baltimore, Maryland
Printed by United Lithographers   New York, New York
Bound by A. Horowitz and Sons   Fairfield, New Jersey
Designed by Christine Kettner
First Edition

Some of these items first appeared in *Cricket: the
magazine for children*; some, in Robert Wallace's
anthologies *Light Year '84, Light Year '85,* and
Light Year '86, all published by Bits Press.
"Electric Blanket Misfortune" by Josh Kennedy
also appeared in *Light Year '86* and is reprinted
by permission of the author.

For Josh Kennedy, early encourager of these verses,
who, bored while his parents shopped, made up this Brat
of his own right there in Filene's bedding department:

Stupid little Lucy Wankett
Washed her automatic blanket
While the thing was still plugged in.
Notify her next of kin.

John while swimming in the ocean
Rubbed sharks' backs with suntan lotion.
Now those sharks have skin of bronze
In their bellies—namely, John's.

Stealing eggs, Fritz ran afoul
Of an angry great horned owl.
Now she has him—what a catch!—
Seeing if his head will hatch.

Vince released a jar of vermin
During Mister Drowser's sermon
On how cheerfulness is catching.
Soon the whole next pew was scratching.

A hiss! A gulp! Where are you, Niles?
Why is your huge pet snake all smiles?
Are you in there, you little dickens,
Where it kind of lumps and thickens?

Doris Drummond sneaked a look
In a locked and cobwebbed book,
Found some secret words you said
That would summon up the dead.
Sad to say, the dead she summoned
Had it in for Doris Drummond.

Thinking it hard candy, Rube
Gobbled down a Rubik's cube.
His stomach, in one revolution,
Came up with the right solution.

Stephanie, that little stinker,
Skinny-dipped in fabric shrinker.
We will find her yet, we hope,
Once we buy a microscope.

Into Mother's slide trombone
Liz let fall her ice cream cone.
Now when marching, Mother drips
Melting notes and chocolate chips.

Louise, a whiz at curling hair,
Sneaked up on a snoozing bear,
Left its fur all frazzly-frizzly.
My, but its revenge was grisly!

At the laundromat Liz Meyer
Flung her brothers in the dryer.
Round and round they've whizzed for years,
Not yet dry behind the ears.

Just because she wants to, Greer
Shoves a snowplow into gear,
Gives a few parked cars a lift.
Greer, you don't quite catch the drift.

Sleeping bag and all, Fritz Fry
Woke to find he'd hit the sky
On the gushing of a geyser.
Don't be such an early riser.

Noticing an open-doored
Spacecraft, Nora sneaked aboard.
Now where is she?
                    Moved, poor dear,
Several million miles from here.

On his motorbike Lars stands
Roaring past us—"Look! no hands!"
Soon with vacant handlebars
Back the bike roars. Look, no Lars!

Hiking in the Rockies, Midge
Meets out on a natural bridge
A long-horned goat. Just one can cross.
Tough luck, Midge: you've lost the toss.

With the garden sprinkler Brett
Drenched the television set
Just to find out: Will flash floods
Turn soap opera to suds?

"Hurry, Doctor! Greedy Greg's
Gobbled all my Easter eggs—
Really, hand-grenades I'd dyed."

"Hmm," says Doc. "Greg, open wide——
Wider——wider——"

BOOOOM!

"Uh-oh.

Guess that's wide as Greg will go."

In the bakery Diane
Poured paint through a whirring fan.
Pass the doughnuts! Pass the crullers!
Pass that pie with flying colors!

On a bet, foolhardly Sam
Leaps inside a mammoth clam,
Bawls, "Boil water! Let's make chowder!"—

SLAM!

Where are you, Sam? Talk louder!

Over Mom's piano keys
Franklin drizzles antifreeze.
Hasn't Mom the hottest keyboard
On the entire eastern seaboard?

Chortling "Ho ho! This'll learn us!"
Gosnold in his grade school's furnace
Hurled a can of kippered herring.
School's been out a whole month, airing.

Camping in Grand Canyon Park,
Bertram, while the sky grew dark
And the first star climbed the sky,
Told a grizzly nine feet high:
"Beat it, b'ar! Don't hang around!
Find your own darned camping ground!"

Sunset grieved, and evening star,
After Bertram crossed the b'ar.

"Lightning? That's an old wives' tale!
Why not swim? Who's scared?" scoffs Hale.

Shortly, bolts that flash like knives
Prove the wisdom of old wives.

Paul, in Aunt Pru's prune surprise,
Plunked two artificial eyes.
Uncle, seeing when he stirred
Someone stare without a word,
Wondered: "How come what Pru cooks
Always gives me glassy looks?"

While we dazed onlookers gawk
Baby's snatched up by a hawk.
Must be few if any chickens
Give that poor bird tougher pickin's.

On the old mill's rotten roof
Gus jumped up and down, the goof,
Quickly down a hole skedaddled.
There he goes round, getting paddled.

For a harmless April rain
Mark mistook a hurricane,
Dashed outside in swimsuit—*whip!*
Up he soared! His sudden trip
From Galveston to Corpus Christi
Left his neck a trifle twisty.

Feeling famished, Lester fried
Fungi pictured in no guide,
Ate—and now that silly dear
Froths green foam from either ear.

Panic struck Flight Nine-Oh-Nine
When DeWitt was heard to whine,
"The wing—it's cracking!"

Little nerd!
He'd only meant his toy Big Bird.

Humbert, hiking Moonshine Hill,
Stumbles on a hidden still.
"Who would like a drink?" he carols——

BAL-AMMM! BAL-AMM!
                     (He gets both barrels.)

Bathing near Oahu, May
Stepped aboard a manta ray.
Where'd it take her?—South Pacific.
Sorry, can't be more specific.

Snickering like crazy, Sue
Brushed a pig with Elmer's Glue
And, to set Aunt Effie squealing,
Stuck it to the kitchen ceiling.
Uncle, gawking, spilled his cup.
"Wow!" he cried. "Has pork gone up!"

While the fruit boils, Mom sends Lars
Out to hunt for jelly jars.
In the twinkling of an eye
Back he bounds with a supply:
Jars in which old Doc McBones
Used to keep folks' kidney stones.
"Lars, you darling!" Mother cries.
"These look perfect! Just the size!"

Only those with steely nerves
Taste Mom's stoneless peach preserves.

Meaning well, Minerva Jean
Picked and cooked but failed to clean
Vegetables. That's why the broccoli
Broke folks' teeth and went down rockily.

In a kangaroo one day
Awful Abner stowed away,
Scrunched himself inside her pocket
Like a lightbulb in a socket.

His foster mother, it appears,
Would not let go of Ab for years
Until he'd passed, like all the rest,
His kangaroo high-jumping test.

Down the blowhole of a whale
Mal poured ice-cold ginger ale.
"Ha!" he chuckled, "there she blows
Tickly bubbles out her nose!"

All at once, two vast tail-slaps
Caused his sailboat to collapse.
After several months the Coast Guard
Dropped Mal's folks a "no luck" postcard.

(Whales are docile beasts unless
Forced to fizz and effervesce.)

At the tennis court, **Paul Pest**
Painted white a hornets' nest.
Father leaped up high to smack it—
Buzzing! Screaming! What a racket!

On Halloween, when ghosts go *boo,*
A lioness escaped her zoo
And Gosnold, meeting her, waxed wise:
"Hey, *I* know *you!* Some cheap disguise!"

He grasped her ears and gave a few
Twists, but her head would not unscrew.
Now Gosnold's well disguised, I guess,
Deep down inside that lioness.

Playing soccer, Plato Foley
Kicked a wasps' nest past the goalie.
Soon the whole crowd jumped up roaring
When those winged things started scoring.

"Mama Bear, you'll never miss
This darling cub!" cooed Beatrice.
"Let me take it for a pet—"

Up a phone pole Bea's treed yet.

Ignatz Mott ignored the rule,
"Never stand behind a mule."

In the sky—what can that be?
Haw haw! *Hee-haw!* That is he.

Gosnold! Watch out with that match
Or the dynamite might catch!

There goes Gosnold: living proof
That a kid can raise the roof.